Merry Christmas William
From Grandma Mary
2015

·STORMIN' NORMAN·

the Soggy Doggy

Written by
Andy Allen

Illustrated by
Brian Barber

ISBN 13: 9781592980390

Library of Congress Catalog Number: 2011939912
Printed in the United States of America
Third Printing: 2014
18 17 16 15 14   7 6 5 4 3

Cover and interior design by Brian Barber
Edited by Kellie Hultgren

Beaver's Pond Press, Inc.
7108 Ohms Lane
Edina, MN 55439-2129
(952) 829-8818
www.BeaversPondPress.com

To order, visit www.BeaversPondBooks.com or call 1-800-901-3480. Reseller discounts available.
For more information visit www.andyandnorm.com

This book belongs to <u>Will</u>

Andy Alben

I am going to sit down to the left of you

And tell you a story I know to be true.

It is a tale of a boy and his dog,

A warm summer's day, a creek, and a log.

The boy's name is Andy, and the dog's name is Norm.

Our story takes place right after a storm.

The rain had been pouring in the Hawkeye State,

'Twas the start of the flood of 2008.

But this day was sunny, the weather was grand.

Andy called Norm with a leash in his hand.

Then Andy set off with his dog by his side,

And his puppy excitement, Norm just could not hide.

Norm jumped and ran and wagged his long tail.

He pranced and he sniffed and he barked at a snail.

The day was beautiful, like out of a dream.

Soon the explorers came across a stream.

Because of the rain the stream ran quite high,

And the friends spied a stick in the water nearby.

Now Norm being a dog, and a curious pup at that,

He sniffed at that stick from the bank where they sat.

After checking the stick out the best that he could,

Well, Norm, he decided to taste that soggy wood.

It looked so delicious, he just had to bite it.

But it was bigger than him, so he had to fight it.

Norm tugged on that stick! He pulled and he yanked,

But then the wood slipped out away from the bank. . . .

The water was high and the current was quick,

But Norm stubbornly stayed attached to that stick.

Andy could see Norm was trying to swim,

But the pup wasn't strong enough to get back to him.

Scared, Norm could hear the shouts of his master,

But the current was getting faster and faster.

Soon Norm had been swept almost out of sight,

So Andy jumped in and swam with all his might.

He plunged in the water, searching for his friend,

But Norm and his stick had gone around the bend.

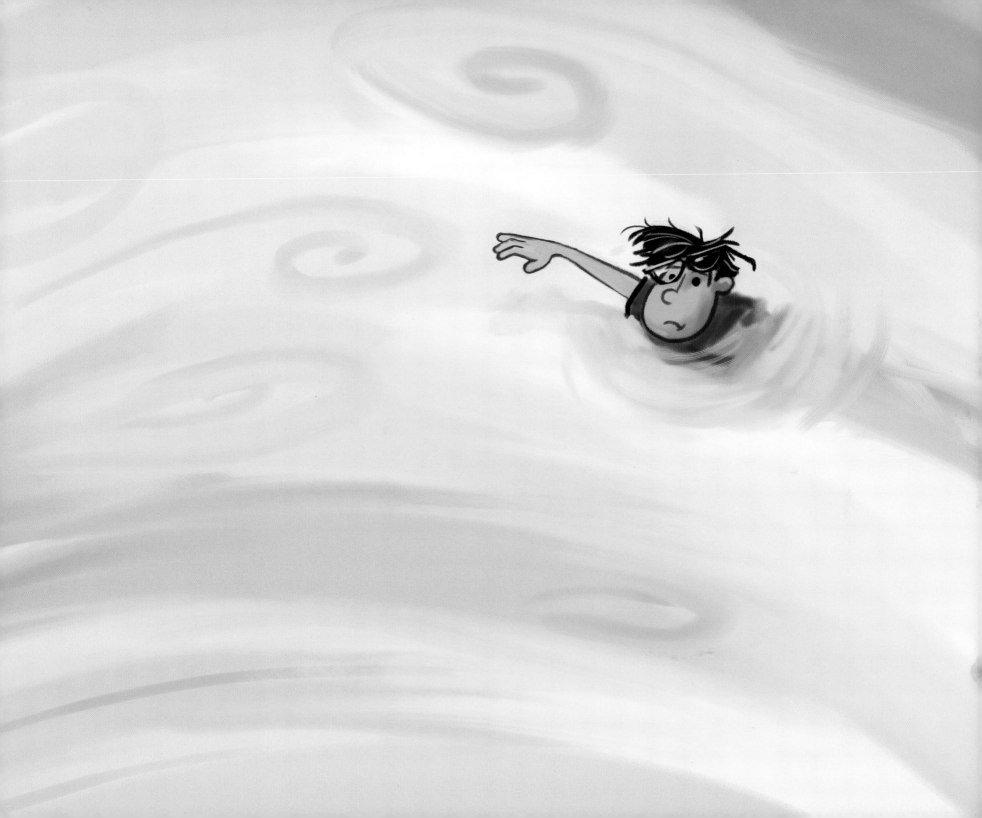

The current was carrying Norm farther south,

And Andy had icky creek water in his mouth.

Through the cold rushing water, he swam to one side.

"Norm, my buddy, where are you?" he cried.

He held onto a rock with a firm grip for sure,

His other hand reached out and felt some wet fur!

With water in his eyes and mud head to toe,

Andy had found Norm—now he wouldn't let go!

He saw Norm and the water locked in quite a tussle,

So he pushed his pal to shore using all of his muscle.

Norm was out and on land, shaking off in no time.

Now it was Andy's turn for the damp climb.

As the tired duo rested safely in the grasses,
Andy realized that he had lost his glasses.

He said, "I guess down there a fish will find a treasure!

With my glasses maybe he can read books for pleasure.

After all, stories are something anyone can enjoy,

Human, or animal, dog, girl, or boy."

"Books can take you on trips and adventures with no end,

Or tell the tale of a boy saving his best friend."

Andy said, "Norm, I'm sure that's how the story goes."

Norm just looked up and kissed him on the nose.

"But Norm, if only you'd have let that stick go by,

Then you and I would have stayed clean, safe, and dry!"

The end.